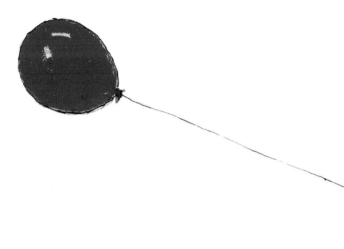

First published in Dutch by Querido under the title *Fabians Feest*
This English edition published by Floris Books in 2018
Text and Illustrations © 2014 Marit Törnqvist
English version © 2018 Floris Books
Marit Törnqvist has asserted her right under the Copyright, Designs
and Patent Act 1988 to be identified as the Author and Illustrator
of this Work. All rights reserved. No part of this publication may be
reproduced without the prior permission of Floris Books, Edinburgh
www.florisbooks.co.uk
British Library CIP Data available
ISBN 978-178250-460-3
Printed in Malaysia

Charlie's Magical Carnival

Marit Törnqvist

Floris
Books

Outside, there was drumming,
and cheering, and trumpeting.
"Mama, I can hear the carnival!
Let's go, it's carnival time!"

But where was Charlie's party hat?
And where was his red balloon?

Mama searched and searched,
while Charlie waited and waited.

"I just thought of something silly," Charlie said.
"What if grown-ups needed training wheels?
Businessmen with training wheels,
old ladies with training wheels…"

"Training wheels?" said Mama,
still looking for the balloon.
Outside, music was playing.
The carnival was in full swing.

"Mama?" said Charlie.
"What if there was a town
with elephants instead of cars?
Fire elephants,
ambulance elephants,
taxi elephants!
Wouldn't that be fun?"

"Mmm, yes… funny," Mama muttered.
She'd found the red balloon,
but where was Charlie's party hat?

"I thought of something else funny, Mama…
What if some people lived in trees?"
Mama was rummaging through drawers.
She wasn't really listening.
"In tree-houses," said Charlie,
"with gardens up high,
way up in the branches,
and all kinds of fancy birds."

"Charlie," Mama sighed,
"please be quiet for a moment.
What with all these trees and fancy birds,
I'll never find your party hat.
Do you want to go to the carnival?"

Be quiet?
No, Charlie *could not* be quiet!
Not today, not with the carnival in town –
the best carnival in the world!
There might be a cake as big as the town square,
lollipop trees and a lemonade river,
marshmallow bunting and cupcake hats.

Charlie couldn't stop talking about
everyone dancing to fast, whirling music,
dogs wearing waistcoats, joining the fun,
fireworks bursting with real shining stars,
and presents tumbling from the skies –
one for every child!

Then Mama shouted very loudly:

"SHUUUUUSSSSHHHH!

Please be quiet, or we won't go at all!"
Charlie stopped talking.
He found his party hat.
Phew. Just in time.

At first the carnival seemed like any other carnival,
just a bit bigger and busier.

But then...

And it did!
They rode through the streets
on their taxi elephant.
Mama was shaking, but only a little.

"Hold on to me, Mama."
Charlie took her hand.

They whirled and
twirled and swirled,
and when they couldn't
dance any longer...

...they stopped to rest on a branch.
The branch of a lollipop tree!
Charlie reached up
and picked them one each.

They licked their lollipops
and dangled their legs as they
watched the carnival below.

Then Charlie remembered…
"The cake!"
They'd forgotten about the cake
as big as the town square!
What if it had all gone?

As fast as they could,
they clambered down
from the treetops.

They reached the town square and –
phew – there was plenty of cake left.
They munched and chewed
and licked their lips
until Mama's dress was tight
and Charlie's tummy was full.

It was very late when they got home.
Mama took off her shoes
and tucked Charlie into bed.

"What an amazing carnival," she said.
"It was much more exciting than usual."
"Which bit did you like best, Mama?" asked Charlie.
Mama yawned.
"It's time for a lovely, long sleep now, Charlie.
Let's talk about it tomorrow."

Charlie snuggled down under his covers.
"Tomorrow's going to be even more fun!"
"What's happening tomorrow?" asked Mama.

Charlie didn't answer.
He was too busy thinking about…

... candy ladders and gingerbread jackets,
a one-man-band with an acrobat dog,
climbing an elephant
and swinging from tusks!

Charlie's magical carnival
was only just beginning.